For Pete – Golden Eagle, storyteller
and teacher extraordinaire – S.P-H.

For Rachel – C.J.

Published in the UK by Scholastic, 2024
1 London Bridge, London, SE1 9BG
Scholastic Ireland, 89E Lagan Road, Dublin Industrial Estate, Glasnevin, Dublin, D11 HP5F

Text © Smriti Prasadam-Halls, 2024
Illustrations © Chris Jevons, 2024

The right of Smriti Prasadam-Halls and Chris Jevons to be identified
as the author and illustrator of this work has been asserted by them under the Copyright,
Designs and Patents Act 1988.

ISBN 978 0702 30958 8

A CIP catalogue record for this book is available from the British Library.

Printed in China.
Paper made from wood grown in sustainable forests and other controlled sources.

1 3 5 7 9 10 8 6 4 2

www.scholastic.co.uk

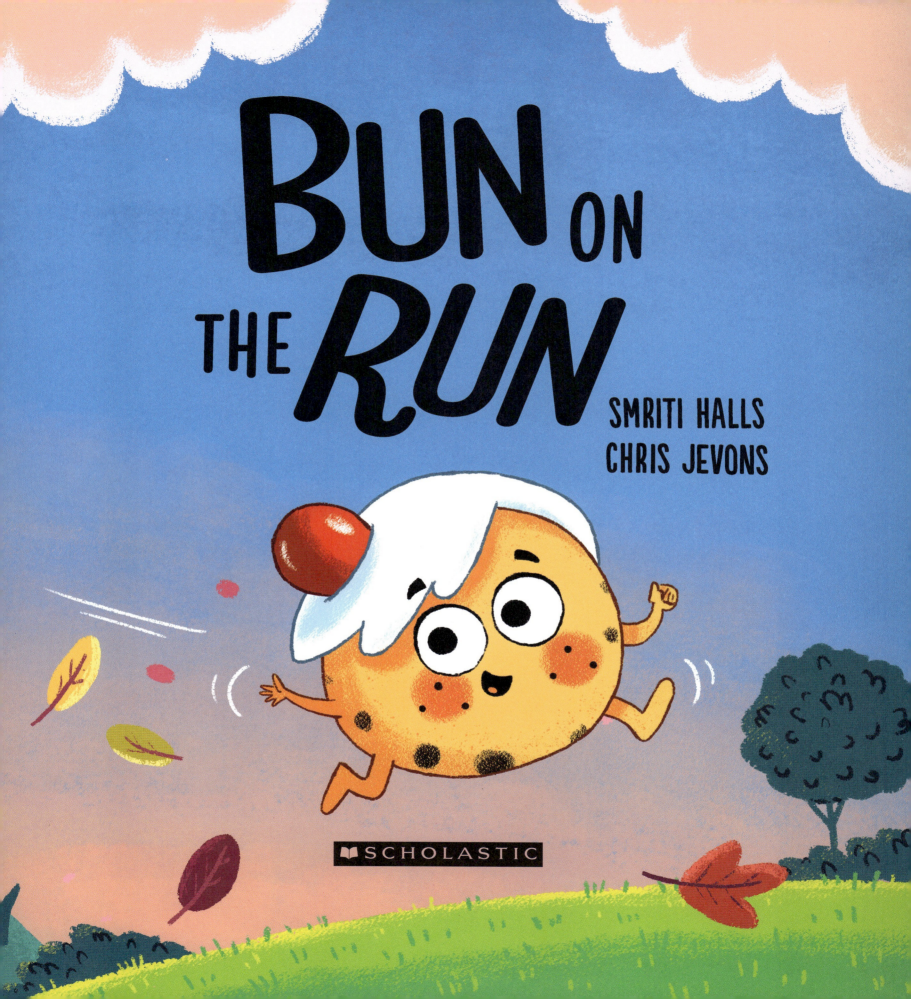

On a shiny white plate in a

BAKER'S SHOP

sat Bernard the bun – with a cherry on top.
He was squidgy and soft,
sugared and spiced,
perfectly round and perfectly iced.

But Bernard had plans and a gleam in his eye,
he waved to his friends, "Goodbye! goodbye!
I've places to go and people to see . . .
there's more to life than THIS for me!"

Bernard hopped down and out of the door,
but what should he see . . .

a big shaggy paw,

a big dribbly mouth
– ready to bite,

six big teeth
– sharp and white!

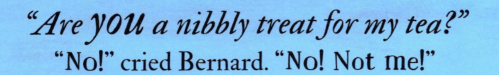

"Are **YOU** a nibbly treat for my tea?"
"No!" cried Bernard. "No! Not me!"

went the dog with
jaws open wide.

Crumbs!

quivered Bernard.
"No time to hide!"

"Wait!" woofed the dog.
"Oh please, won't you stay?"

"NOT ON YOUR NELLY!

Nope, no way!

You can chase, chase, chase,
you can run, run, run,

But you can't catch me,
I'm Bernard the bun!"

But just down the path was
a nasty surprise . . .

two twitchy ears

and two twinkly eyes.

A well brushed tail
and soft, silky fur,

"Oooh what have we here?"
came a soft, silky purr.

"Are **YOU** a nibbly treat
for my tea?"

"No!" cried Bernard. "No! Not me!"

Meow! went the cat and got ready to pounce, Bernard the bun went **bounce** . . .

bounce . . .

bounce!

"*Wait!*" purred the cat.
"*Oh please, won't you stay?*"

"NOT ON YOUR NELLY!
Nope, no way!

You can race, race, race,
you can run, run, run,

But you can't catch me,
I'm Bernard the bun!"

Over the gate jumped
Bernard the bun.
He skipped in the
meadow, he danced in
the sun.

"Wait!" honked the goose.
"Oh please, won't you stay?"

"NOT ON YOUR NELLY!

Nope, no way!

You can hop, hop, hop, you can run, run, run,

But you can't catch me, I'm Bernard the bun!"

"At last," thought Bernard.
"Hurray! I'm free!
What a LUCKY little bun
I've managed to be."

"I escaped from a goose
and a dog and a cat.
All by myself!
Well how about that!"

"Now I've run and I've run,
what I need is a nap . . ."

But just at that moment
a beak went . . .

SNAP!

Bernard the bun sailed high in the air.
This wasn't right! This wasn't fair!
It didn't look good – that much was true . . .
whatever was a little iced bun meant to do?

Bernard thought hard, "I know just the thing!"
He cleared his throat
. . . and started to sing.

"You can flap, flap, flap,
you can run, run, run,
But you can't catch me,
I'm *Bernard the bun!*"

"TOO LATE!"

cawed the crow, but as she started to speak . . .

Bernard the bun tumbled
out of her beak!

"Goodbye *silly* crow!" giggled Bernard. "Yippee!
I've got places to go
and people to see . . ."

So Bernard the bun ran far, far away . . .
if you're lucky, you might even spot him one day!

And since Bernard had vanished to goodness-knows-where,
the dog . . .
    the cat . . .
        the goose . . .
           and the crow . . .

. . . chased Charlie the chocolate éclair!